LOVE BETRAYS YOU

CONNOR WHITELEY

No part of this book may be reproduced in any form or by any electronic or mechanical means. Including information storage, and retrieval systems, without written permission from the author except for the use of brief quotations in a book review.

This book is NOT legal, professional, medical, financial or any type of official advice.

Any questions about the book, rights licensing, or to contact the author, please email connorwhiteley@connorwhiteley.net

Copyright © 2024 CONNOR WHITELEY

All rights reserved.

DEDICATION
Thank you to all my readers without you I couldn't do what I love.

CHAPTER 1
6th May 2023
Rochester, England

MI5 Intelligence Officer Marcus Dawson had sat on his favourite grey camping chair with just the right levels of support in all the right places as he sat to one side of the huge football in front of him. The large thick white lines of the pitch had been freshly painted and even though he knew next to nothing about football he still loved helping out.

Marcus smiled as he watched his big brother, Ryan, run about in his bright blue football jersey with tons of little eight-year-olds kids running after him and after the football at the same time.

He had to admit that the weather was perfect for a Saturday morning kick about and coaching session. Marcus wasn't really sure why his brother had wanted the help because Ryan had always been brilliant with kids, but if it meant he got to see more of his brother between "business trips" then he certainly wasn't going to complain at all.

The day was crisp and warm and the bright sunshine bathed the football in a perfect golden light that really made Marcus smile. It was a perfect summer day and he hadn't received a single call from MI5 for a few days, so hopefully everything was right with the world.

Or as right as they could be when you had Russia, China and the middle east all looking for any weakness in the UK to exploit. Some days Marcus couldn't decide if the UK's enemies were just being stupid or they were just useless at their jobs.

It wasn't exactly hard to find a weakness in the UK.

Marcus smiled as the smell aromas of sausage rolls, pizza and tacos filled the air from the nearby food truck that always set up shop behind him in the car park. He was so looking forward to having lunch with his brother and they could catch up about Ryan, his wife and their three beautiful children.

Marcus would have loved to have a kid or boyfriend of his own but that was the problem with intelligence work, it was flat out impossible to meet people. And it was even harder to stay together. It was normally the secrets, the lies and the tension from the missions that always killed a relationship in the end.

"Watch out," someone said.

Marcus moved his head slightly as a football flew past him.

Marcus laughed, got the ball and kicked it back onto the football pitch. It was so worth helping out just so he could see the grins and shouts of happiness from the little kids.

They really did love it here.

"So this is what you do when you don't want to come to work," a woman said behind him.

Marcus smiled as he turned around and saw his best friend in the entire world and handler, Madame Aria Roaings. Marcus couldn't deny she looked great in her long black trench coat, black hat and black high heels. She had to be baking inside given the heat of the late morning but Marcus was never going to argue with her.

"It's nice you still keep in touch with your brother," Aria said.

Marcus wanted to hug her but he didn't dare. Aria was way too emotionless and cold for that to happen. He still didn't like being reminded of how Aria's kids and entire family and husband believed she had died years ago in a plane crash.

It was simply safer that way for everyone and it meant she could move a lot more freely in the shadows of the world.

"I love my brother and I take it you're not going to let me enjoy lunch with him," Marcus said knowing the answer already.

Aria allowed a rare smile to crack her lips. "Of course I'll allow you but I thought you might want the extra time to prepare for an important task. And I hope you own a tux,"

Marcus grinned. He always loved missions that required him to dress up, it wasn't so much so that he liked looking amazing himself. It was more the fact that if he needed to dress up nicely then so did a lot of other insanely hot men.

Men in suits looked sensational. Marcus was always hard at the thought of it.

"What's the job?" Marcus asked waving at Ryan as he ran past with the kids just chasing him now.

"Two days ago the UK's latest advancement in communication jamming software was stolen. It's called Blackout for a reason and-"

Marcus nodded. "I've heard of the software before. Can it really Blackout all of the US if placed and activated in the right location?"

"Exactly," Aira said. "Every single TV screen, telephone, mobile phone and more across the entire USA could be knocked out for days if Blackout was activated. And that means a hell of a lot of European countries could be knocked out too,"

"I think it's safe to presume that is not the reason we're going after Blackout," Marcus said smiling because he knew full well the UK Government couldn't have cared less about mainland Europe.

"True," Aria said smiling as a kid ran past, stopped to look at her and then ran off again.

"Where am I going then?"

"There's a party tonight in Canterbury being hosted by one of the top families in the UK and it's an auction for Blackout. All the various Intelligence services and terrorism organisations throughout the world will be there to get their hands on it,"

"You need me to go in there, get Blackout and kill whoever took it in the first place," Marcus said.

"Negative. Get Blackout get out. We cannot kill anyone at that party because it is too high profile. Blackout is my only concern and I'll send you the details of what it looks like in a moment. Can you handle it?"

Marcus laughed. He could always handle a simple retrieval mission. Marcus couldn't believe it would be that hard to go into a mansion or wherever the party was being held, get Blackout out without anyone realising and simply slip back into the night.

It wasn't hard.

But Marcus was looking forward to seeing all those hot sexy men in their tight black suits a lot more than he ever wanted to admit.

Tonight was going to be a lot of fun.

CHAPTER 2
6th May 2023
Canterbury, England

Aden Grant didn't exactly consider himself a bad person, a bad man or something who enjoyed anything about his father's family business. He saw himself as more of a "getting the job done" sort of man and given how his father had fostered him, adopted him and given him everything when his own parents had abandoned him as a child.

Aden really didn't see the harm in simply getting a few slightly illegal items for his father.

He took a wonderfully cool crystal glass of champagne as the hot male waiter in his very tight black suit came round the immense circular hall the guests had been stuffed into. It was hardly the best, but not the worst, party he had ever been to.

Aden rather liked the seriously tall white textured walls that reminded him of chapels and various religious buildings that might have been crappy, but even hateful religion can be beautiful at times.

High above the guests was a beautiful chandelier that Aden had never really been fussed with before, but there was just something about how this one was shining like diamonds high in the ceiling, that he really liked. Then he realised the chandelier did have diamonds on it and if the hall was a little less empty he might have actually tried to steal them.

He never knew when his father might need some diamonds for the business.

Aden nodded his hellos to a very cute man in a slightly loose-fitting black suit with a blond beard, brown shoes and a beautiful smile. The entire hall might have been packed with hot straight men but Aden couldn't deny the fact everyone looked beautiful in their suits.

And even the slim, cold and more probably assassin women attached to their arms looked very attractive to. They all had their blue, red and black dresses and Aden wasn't sure if the women in their dresses were trying to stand out or not.

He was definitely going to have to focus on them because it was only the sexist "official" government agencies that believed women were weak and stupid. Aden seriously knew from personal experience that women were a lot more dangerous than men when it came to these sorts of events.

And Aden had already recognised at least twenty internationally wanted criminals here and another forty intelligence officers from all over the world. It seemed that everyone wanted Blackout but Aden wasn't going to let that happen.

Only he was walking away from Blackout.

"And who are you?"

Aden looked around to see a rather pretty young woman in a black dress standing there, he knew her. Why his father had sent Isabella along too was a pain in the neck. He loved her as a foster sister but this wasn't right. This was his mission, his right and his chance to prove himself.

"Relax little bro," Isabella said taking his champagne glass and downing it in one. "Father trusts you. He really does but Blackout is too important to let slip so we are working together,"

"You make that sound like a bad thing,"

Isabella smiled. "The one that shot me in the ass last year,"

Aden laughed. He still had no idea how he had managed that but now she had mentioned it, Aden focused on the way that everyone was walking.

It was a little-known fact that even the most powerful, experienced and lethal intelligence officers always moved slightly differently depending on whether they were packing a gun or not, or even knives.

Aden always preferred knives to guns because they were a lot more fun and exciting and interesting, but it seemed everyone else here was a lot more interested in guns.

"I do have a spare Glock if you want it," Isabella

said.

"You know I don't do guns,"

Isabella laughed. "And one day that will be the death of you little brother. Now I will leave you because we need to keep our association unknown and if someone else wins flirt and get with them,"

"Of course but what if it's a woman?"

"Really?" Isabella asked laughing. "You're gay and most of these people are straight. You were always doing to have to get with a woman tonight,"

"What about you getting with a man?"

Isabella grinned that maddening smile that made Aden's stomach churn and curdle. "Apparently I'm too scary for hookups,"

Aden smiled because he didn't doubt that for a second considering she always killed her boyfriends in short order.

He watched her walk away and he noticed there was a new person coming into the hall and-

Wow. Fuck. Fuck. Fuck.

Aden seriously wished he had a glass of champagne to down it the moment as he watched the most sensational, explosive, divine man he had ever met in his entire life stalk into the hall.

He had never seen a man with such confidence, such power and authority just walk into a hall and seem to dominate it. And the man in his extremely hot, sexy black suit that showed off his fit ass and his sexy insanely seductive body, Aden just didn't know what to do.

He was glued in place.

Aden wanted to run, hide or even go over and talk to the hottie but his body wasn't listening.

The man's face was insanely hot as Aden just focused on him. His strong jawline, short brown hair and his lifeful and hopeful eyes were so stunning Aden never wanted to look away.

Now Aden just hoped beyond hope that the mere presence of this hottie wasn't going to distract him because he had to get Blackout for his father no matter the cost.

So the best way to make sure the hottie didn't get Blackout was to make sure Aden was with him when the auction started.

And the hottie was alone so he might even be gay.

Aden just grinned at that amazing idea because that seriously would be sensational.

CHAPTER 3
6th May 2023
Canterbury, England

As Marcus went into the immense hall where the party and auction was happening he was certainly glad the hot, sexy men of the world's various intelligence services and criminal underworld had maintained their part of the bargain about looking hot in their nice tight black suits.

Intelligence officers and criminals seriously knew how to dress up great when they wanted to.

Marcus smiled at a young waitress as she passed him a glass of champagne, he had no intention of drinking it but it was all part of the show. It was good seeing so many old intelligence friends, both male and female, and old enemies in their suits and dresses.

The bright chandelier above looked wonderful and it made Marcus smile as he remembered fun missions in Italy, Spain and a whole bunch of other catholic countries with their stunning architecture. He didn't get to travel much because MI5 was only focused on the UK's internal security but every so often he got to travel abroad.

Something that he loved with all his heart.

The only feature of the hall he didn't like was the weird textured white walls, they just looked weird and out of place. Something was wrong with them but Marcus couldn't put his finger on it.

A group of women walked past Marcus and he just didn't understand them.

Marcus had no idea why the women wanted to wear bright red dresses because surely that would only draw attention to them. Or maybe that was the point, the eyes focused on the women in red dresses whilst the women in black dresses actually got the work done and stole Blackout.

He wasn't exactly sure how many of the people here tonight actually intended to steal Blackout or simply just pay for it like they were meant to. Marcus didn't want to pay for it because the UK Government would never have the money for it.

The country was broke as fuck after all, Marcus really couldn't understand why the UK should have to pay for their own equipment back?

It made no sense.

"There's half the criminal underworld in here," Jessica said in his earpiece.

Marcus was really glad that Jessica had given up her Saturday night to support him back at HQ and she was currently watching the room through a camera in one of his buttons.

"I know," Marcus said quietly, "just talk me through it all and I'll nod or something,"

"Look over there to your left. The man with the half-burnt head of hair. That is a Syrian militant leader wanted in fifty countries for terrorism, murder and genocide,"

Marcus nodded. He might want to take him out if given the chance.

"Then to your right if you look at the large elderly woman who is the director of the Chilean Security Service and she will kill everyone if she gets the chance,"

Marcus wasn't too bothered about her.

"And the man coming towards you is a nobody. There is no official record of him," Jessica said.

Marcus looked straight ahead and… oh. He seriously had a feeling that this mission was going to be fucked in short order.

Marcus could only stare with his mouth open at the utterly beautiful, stunning and outrageously hot man walking towards him so artfully, gracefully and silently that Marcus didn't doubt he was a perfect assassin.

It was fascinating and beautiful to watch the man glide through the crowd without touching, talking or disrupting a single person in the tightly packed room. And yet Marcus could see him and he was so beautiful.

Marcus wasn't sure exactly what made him so

stunning. It might have been his perfectly pointy jaw and his handsome face that made him all so young, baby-faced and cute. It could have been his fit as fuck body that didn't show any signs of muscles, body fat or anything.

But the guy was carrying a weapon.

He was walking too silently and gracefully for it to be a gun so Marcus was willing to bet knives. It was old-fashioned for sure but Marcus couldn't deny if a young man like himself was cool enough to enough knives instead of a gun then he was certainly a man worth talking too.

Marcus almost felt like a giant compared to the man as he walked a metre from him.

"You saw me," the man said in a deep, manly sexy voice. "Not a lot of people are able to see me through crowds."

"Not a lot of people carry knives these days. I prefer a Glock myself," Marcus said.

The man started walking circles around him and again the entire groups of people around him simply moved like they were being moved by a force they didn't know was affecting them.

"A Glock is too powerful, too quick, too loud," the man said. "Knives are quieter, more skilful and they get the job done. You have to be MI5?"

Marcus laughed. This man was good and really hot and beautiful.

"And before you ask it's the suit that gave you away. It is not an expensive Italian suit like a lot of what these men are wearing,"

"You aren't wearing silk either. Are you a government officer?"

Marcus didn't know why the beautiful man was laughing so much. It was a good question.

"Heavens no," the man said looking around so Marcus guessed he wasn't alone.

"Relax," Jessica said. "I'm looking through the camera footage now to see if anyone else is focusing on the man. Find out his name,"

"I'm Marcus. What about you?"

"Your government databases don't have me on there?" the man said offering Marcus his hand. "My name's Aden,"

Marcus took the man's hand and was seriously surprised by how warm, smooth and wonderful it was as he felt affection, chemistry and even a little sexual tension flow between them.

Then Aden flicked the suit button containing the camera and Marcus frowned as he knew the camera was broken.

"Shall we attend the auction?" Aden asked offering Marcus his arm.

Marcus had no idea at all who the hell this man was but he was beautiful, a little crazy and Marcus supposed as he was after Blackout too, Marcus really had to keep this hottie a lot closer than he normally would.

And that was hardly a problem at all.

CHAPTER 4
6th May 2023
Canterbury, England

Aden hadn't exactly intended to run into an MI5 officer whilst at the party but he was more than glad he had. Marcus had to be the hottest, most beautiful man he had ever seen and for someone from MI5 he was clearly intelligent. Something the officers he tended to come across seriously lacked.

Aden loved how smooth, warm and natural having Marcus on his arm felt. It had been a lot longer than Aden wanted to admit since he had time with a hot man and at least gotten the chance to show him off in public.

He led Marcus towards the very front of the hall were a small white stage had been erected and a podium was already up ready for the auction to begin. Everyone else in their blue, black and red dresses and sexy suits were tightly packed together because everyone was just waiting for the shit to hit the fan.

The entire problem with the hall was that there were only two exits. It wouldn't be hard for an enemy operative to secure them and then just kill them all and Aden really didn't like being limited by his options.

Aden subtly moved a hand down to his waist where he kept his knives because everything was very off here. There was a poor smell of sweat, fear and damp that clung to the air and made the awful taste of sweaty gym socks form on his tongue from where his real brothers used to bully him as a child.

Aden looked at beautiful Marcus and he just grinned at how cute he was. It was clear Marcus had worked out the same as him but it was probably because his tech support person couldn't see what they were seeing. He hadn't really meant to destroy the camera but he just had to protect his father, the family business and Isabella.

They had given him everything and he just wanted to protect them.

Then Aden noticed every single person in the room was subtly moving their hands towards their weapons.

"This is a setup," Aden said quietly to Marcus.

"By who and what would they want to gain?"

Aden smiled. "You have the world's top intelligence officers in these walls and the other half of the world's top criminals. Attack here and a hell of a lot of organisations become headless,"

"You still haven't told me who you work for?"

Aden was so tempted to reveal small parts of himself to this hot, beautiful man but that would be a deadly mistake. He couldn't afford to get attached, he couldn't afford love, he couldn't afford anything to do with Marcus.

But he would keep him alive for now.

"I don't see Blackout," Marcus said.

Aden waved him silent as an elderly woman went onto the stage wearing a sweeping blue dress and she stood at the podium.

"My dearest intelligence officers and wonderful criminals," the woman said. "I didn't want it to come to this but I have changed by mind about selling Blackout because it is simply too much fun to use,"

A whole bunch of criminals whipped out their guns. Aden had to admit the woman and the criminals were stupid unless the woman had a plan he hadn't figured out yet.

The woman unveiled her dress sleeves a little and revealed a large black watch containing all sorts of flashing lights, transmitters and God knows what. But that was Blackout or at least it was the control mechanism that the rest of Blackout ran off.

Whoever controlled that watch controlled the entire system.

Aden heard a lot of people at the back of the room shut the doors and seal them. Everyone else hadn't noticed it yet and he had to protect his family and Isabella and Marcus.

They had to get out now. This was a clusterfuck

and a half because everyone was about to get murdered.

"We have to go," Aden said.

Marcus whipped out his gun. "Not without Blackout. I have a mission,"

"Leave it. There's always another way. Don't die for nothing," Aden said taking out a knife.

He really didn't know a way out of here but through the crowds to their left about twenty metres away there was a second way out. The same way the woman had entered the stage from.

It was their only way.

"And just so no one can come after me as I set the world on fire you are all going to die," the woman said grinning.

Aden threw a knife at her.

It slammed into her chest.

Aden flicked his wrist and the tiny string on the knife made it fly back to him.

The entire hall went silent.

And the silence was replaced with the sound of a dragon roaring.

Missiles were incoming.

CHAPTER 5
6th May 2023
Canterbury, England

As much as Marcus flat out didn't know anything about beautiful Aden he really didn't want him to die.

The deafening roar of the incoming missiles roared overhead and Marcus grabbed the beautiful man next to him. They had to escape, get out of there and just forget about Blackout for now. Their lives were way too important.

Three missiles ripped into the building.

Marcus's ears rang.

Chunks of ceiling smashed down around them.

The chandelier shattered. Smashing down onto the floor.

People collapsed to the ground.

Marcus saw tons of people swarming towards the stage.

Machine guns fired.

Flames exploded everywhere.

A large group of men stormed out of the second entrance towards the murdered woman. They were going to retrieve Blackout.

Aden was about to throw a knife. Marcus grabbed his wrist.

"They're distracted. We leave now," Marcus said.

Aden rolled his eyes. A woman tackled Marcus to the ground.

He landed on a corpse.

The woman wrapped her hands round his throat. He recognised her. She was an old enemy.

A knife slammed into her head.

Marcus kicked the corpse off him.

More machine gun fire ripped through the audience.

Chunks of ceiling smashed down around them.

Flames poured from the ceiling.

Marcus charged.

Aden followed him.

Some of the machine gun men noticed.

Marcus fired his Glock.

Bullets screamed through the air.

Chests exploded.

Marcus went through the second entrance. He didn't know where he was going. He simply kept running down the silver corridor.

Marcus hooked a right.

Three women in black dresses jumped out. Firing pistols.

Marcus leapt to one side behind a kitchen door.

He fired blind. The women went to reload and Marcus looked out again ready to fire but Aden had already killed them all with his knives.

Marcus went over to Aden who was standing oddly close to the bodies pulling out his knives and Marcus had to admit he was impressed.

And now that he was finally standing behind Aden, Marcus definitely wasn't going to lie about how amazing Aden's ass looked in that nice tight suit.

Marcus aimed his Glock out ahead of them as him and Aden continued down the corridor and the icy cold draft and aroma of smoke and charred flesh told him that the exit was up ahead.

"What the hell happened here?" Marcus asked.

"I don't know. My father's organisation was simply requested to come here and was given the chance to bid on the item,"

Marcus shook his head. "They played us all for fools and idiots. I bet everyone in that damn room got a tip-off and it was a planned slaughter,"

Marcus checked an opening in the corridor for more enemies but it was empty and he noticed a large steel door ahead was open. Almost trying to lure them outside.

"We have to find out who the hell stole Blackout in the first place," Marcus said, "and then get it back,"

He heard Aden laugh behind him.

"What's so funny?" Marcus asked.

"That's MI5 job. My job's failed for now because I only wanted to come here tonight to get Blackout myself. I'm chasing nothing and come on this organisation clearly has money and resources,"

Marcus was about to comment when he heard footsteps run up behind him.

Marcus spun around. Silly Aden was frozen.

The woman fired.

Marcus tackled Aden.

Marcus ducked into a small storage room. Using the door as cover.

He fired. Again. Again.

The woman kept charging.

Marcus jumped out into the woman's rampage.

He saw her.

He fired.

She went down.

Thankfully he was okay and then he checked on beautiful Aden. He really hoped that he was okay and he wasn't injured. He knew he had only just met this beautiful man but Marcus really did want to see him more and more.

Aden smiled on the floor and then just stood up like nothing had ever happened.

"You know if you want to touch me you only have to ask. You don't need to tackle me to the ground,"

Marcus laughed and him and the beautiful man next to him simply went out of the steel door and out onto the cobblestone high street of Canterbury walking away from the ugly noise of police, counterterrorism and fire engine sirens.

After walking in silence for a few moments Marcus looked at Aden and pinned him up against the wall.

"Who are you?" Marcus asked.

He didn't trust him in the slightest and as much as Marcus just wanted to kiss and hug the stunning man something had happened tonight and Marcus had a feeling Aden knew a lot more than he was letting on.

"Why didn't you dive to one side when that woman attacked us?" Marcus asked. "You have the skills to notice something bad was about to happen in the hall but not when a woman is storming towards us,"

Aden grinned and kissed Marcus.

Marcus jumped in shock but he didn't stop the kiss. He didn't resist, he just enjoyed it and allowed the amazing mind-blowing feeling of Aden's full, tasty lips flow between them.

Aden seriously knew how to kiss.

Then Aden flipped himself over Marcus's shoulder so Marcus was now pinned against the wall.

"As much as I love intelligence games I have a family to get back to but I hope to see you again dearest Officer Marcus," Aden said giving him another kiss.

Marcus just turned around and watched Aden and his wonderful ass walk away off into the night. He had no idea who this man was but he was certainly beautiful, certainly clever and certainly up to something.

And that excited Marcus a lot more than he ever wanted to admit.

CHAPTER 6
6th May 2023
Canterbury, England

Aden was seriously not impressed that damn Isabella had tried to shoot at him and sexy Marcus. Of course the bullets weren't real, her death wasn't real and everything about the damn scene was fake as anything. But the attacked and murdered bodies they were very real and clearly whoever was behind all of this knew exactly what they were.

Aden went into the little apartment in the heart of Canterbury they were using as their safehouse for tonight only. It didn't exactly have a lot of stuff and Aden was wearing thick rubber gloves to avoid leaving any prints and tomorrow before they left they would clean the place so none of their DNA remained.

Aden looked at the black sofa, ugly wooden dining table with a wobbly leg and single still-standing dining chair and he just went to sit on it. The other dining chair had broken early because Isabella had sat on it whilst she was cleaning her Glock, Aden had laughed and she had only smiled.

It was those little moments that Aden loved about his family, because he was part of something and it was nice that his family respected him, loved him and wanted to support him no matter what.

The awful smell of rotten meat, rotten vegetables and cat wee filled the air as Isabella came out from the bathroom. And Aden was going to be so glad to get rid of this place tomorrow but they had still failed.

Aden wasn't sure what the plan was now. They could easily go out again and try to find out what was happening with Blackout and try again. Or Aden wasn't sure if Father already had another job for them so he needed them back sooner rather than later.

Isabella just grinned at him as she sat on the dining table.

"It's a shame he didn't shoot you," Aden said smiling.

Aden went over and hugged Isabella because it was good that she was okay but he would have rather she hadn't seen him with Marcus. The last thing he ever wanted her to believe was that Marcus was his weakness.

Aden wasn't sure if he was but he was so cute, innocent and handsome that Aden really wanted to spend more time with him.

"What now?" Aden asked. "I killed the woman but what happened to Blackout?"

Isabella grinned. "The machine gun idiots dealt with everyone else. You, me and your boy toy were the only survivors so the organisation the woman controlled has Blackout back,"

Aden hated it how she called Marcus his boy toy. He wouldn't have minded at all if that was the case but they had a job to focus on.

"We have to call Father," Aden said, "we need to get permission to pursue this. He might have something else lined up,"

"Negative," Isabella said icy cold. "Father might not tell us everything but we both know our missions are our own. He never sends two of us together unless it is critical,"

"Fine," Aden said rolling his eyes and his stomach filled with butterflies at the very idea of seeing beautiful Marcus again.

Isabella got out her smartphone.

"What you searching up?" Aden asked doing the same and looking at the local media reports of the attack.

"There's only one location in the entire Canterbury area where a missile area could be launched from without the Navy getting called,"

"Impossible," Aden said before realising what she meant. "You mean this was launched from the outskirts of Canterbury,"

"And the police have already found a burnt-out truck and missile launchers have been recovered. Military grade," Isabella said.

Aden shook his head. He might have been a criminal and he had seen some amazing equipment in his family business from time to time but launching military-grade missiles, that was brave and stupid.

And this organisation clearly had money to burn.

"What are you looking up you never answered?"

"Oh sorry," Isabella asked. "I'm looking up any criminal organisation that wasn't there tonight,"

Aden had to admit that was really clever. He didn't know Isabella actually had that in her. Then he realised something he should have seen earlier.

"The crystal champagne glasses. There is only one criminal organisation in the entire underworld and international markets that only serve things in crystal.

"The Crystal Dragons," Isabella said, "and I didn't recognise anyone from that group tonight. And normally I always have a talk with Tyler,"

Aden shook his head. Tyler Cha was as fucking hot and twisted as the next serial killer but the Crystal Dragons specialised in murder, kidnapping and drugs but it was their ethical code that made Aden partly trust them.

A mass murder event was ballsy even by the Dragons standards but they had never used military-grade equipment before, they believed it only bought more trouble than it was worth.

"Where is Tyler?" Aden asked.

"London," Isabell asked. "You go up there in case you run into your Boy Toy and I'll see what my other contacts can learn in the shadows. Just be fun little brother,"

Aden hugged her and he couldn't deny that a little voice in the pit of his stomach was telling him something was extremely wrong. His sister was many things but she was never this supportive and nice to him.

She had to be working an angle and that angle terrified him a lot more than he ever wanted to admit.

CHAPTER 7
7th May 2023
London, England

Of all the reactions Marcus had expected MI5 to have last night when he eventually reported in, it definitely hadn't been a strange type of relief that most of the world's corrupt, twisted criminals and enemy intelligence officers were now dead. It wasn't exactly a weird reaction because Marcus imagined he would feel the same if he was in charge, but it still unnerved him.

Thankfully Jessica had noticed a dragon sign at the bottom of the champagne glasses used at the party, and as much as Marcus didn't want to have to deal with the Crystal Dragons because they were foul, evil murderers. He really did have to talk to them and confirm if they were behind the attack or not.

Leading him to the Dragon Pink Club in London.

Marcus leant against a warm sticky brown wall of

the club with a white towel loosely wrapped around his waist. The club was a gay sex sauna in the heart of London that specialised in serving the Leader of the Crystal Dragons, Tyler.

Marcus focused on the immense steam room he was standing in. Large columns of endless steam rose up from the floor boards, there was even a small pool in the middle of the room where two very hot young men were making out.

That was really hot to see.

The club itself was packed with tons of gay men of all different weights, heights and types. Marcus really did like looking at all the men because they were so hot and stunning to look at.

But none of them were as hot as Aden. None of these men had his natural beauty, his effortlessly fit body and his artful movements. Marcus would have loved to see him again but he doubted that was going to happen. He didn't know what he would have given up to have another kiss, another touch and just another chance to spend time with that hot man but he would have given up something.

He really, really wanted to see that beautiful man again.

"Tyler," a very young man said as he walked round naked. He had to be one of the waiters. "Your room is ready per your request and you have a guest,"

Marcus carefully went through the crowd of hot sexy young men around him and he went closer to where the voices were coming from.

He noticed there was a very tall Chinese man standing about ten metres from him with a golden towel wrapped around his very fit waist. He was smiling at the young man and he seemed like he was completely alone.

But Marcus wasn't stupid enough to believe that.

"Who is the guest?" Tyler asked.

"A man that did not want to be identified by his organisation only his first name is Aden," the waiter said.

Marcus shook his head. His stomach twisted into a painful knot as he realised he was finally going to see the beautiful man he wanted to do a lot of stuff to, but he couldn't get over the fact that Aden had such easy access to some of the most dangerous criminals on the planet.

Who the hell was Aden?

"That will be fine. I trust Aden and his father's organisation please tell the men to stand down," Tyler said as he went through a glass door into another steam room.

Marcus really wished he had Jessica with him so she could look at the building schematics but he had sort of looked at them earlier.

Through that door it was a long steamed corridor with a private room at the very end of it so that had to be were Aden and Tyler were meeting.

Marcus carefully glided through the crowd to get to the steamed door. He wished had a gun or something with him but he couldn't hide as much as he used to under a towel.

He went through the glass door and he was almost blinded by the sheer heat and stickiness and steam that covered his vision.

He heard footsteps come towards him.

He ducked.

A fist rushed past him.

Marcus leapt up.

Punching the guy in the chin.

He slipped.

Smashing his head on the wall.

The steam was deactivated.

The steam turned to rain.

Three men charged at him.

Marcus flew forward.

Punching one man in-between the legs.

He screamed. He fell to the floor.

Marcus jumped on his head. It cracked.

Another man kicked Marcus in the chest.

Marcus slipped.

He didn't hit his head.

The man climbed on top of Marcus.

Wrapping his hands round his throat.

Marcus punched the man's elbows.

He fell forward.

Marcus leapt up.

Climbed on him.

Snapped the man's neck.

Then Marcus stopped as he heard the cold cocking of a pistol behind him. He slowly turned around and frowned as the third man was armed and gestured Marcus to get on his knees.

Something flew through the air and the man's corpse landed with a thud a moment later.

"It seems that I have to keep saving you," Aden said at the end of the corridor. "You might want to reattach your towel before you come and join us. Very good though,"

Marcus shook his head and grinned as he realised he had lost his towel in the fight but it was good to know Aden liked his body. And now all Marcus wanted to know was what Aden's body looked like under that very short towel of his.

He really hoped he was about to find out.

CHAPTER 8
7th May 2023
London, England

Aden was so damn excited that Marcus was finally here and he had actually seen the stunning, sexy man in his full glory. Aden couldn't believe that not only was Marcus insanely fit under his clothes but he was rather nicely hung under his towel too.

He couldn't deny that he was a little nervous about his own manly parts in comparison but Aden was just glad to have the wonderful man he seriously liked joining him. And it was the perfect way to monitor what the intelligence services were doing without tipping his hand.

Aden went back into the large brown steam room where Tyler was laying butt-naked on a massage table with a small wooden table next to him filled with all sorts of scented oils, lube and condoms. Aden wasn't sure if Tyler normally got fucked every Sunday morning but he was determined to fuck him in a nonphysical way.

Tyler had information for him and Aden was more than determined to get it. There wasn't a chance in hell that Tyler was getting out of his room alive unless he helped Aden get closer to the location of Blackout.

Aden smiled as beautiful Marcus came into the steam room and he laughed a little that he was surprised to see Tyler butt-naked in front of him.

Aden went over to Tyler and gently ran a finger down his rather fit body all the way to the bottom of the spine and the associated pressure points.

Aden pressed on them.

"Ouch!" Tyler shouted.

"Now then my dear," Aden said," the Crystal Dragons attempted to assassinate me last night. We both know my father wouldn't appreciate that, and Isabella was also there,"

"We did no such thing,"

"Liar," Marcus said. "I was there too and your symbol is on all the crystal champagne glasses,"

Aden was impressed MI5 was intelligent enough to find the marking he had missed. It made him like Marcus even more if such a thing was possible.

"Fine," Tyler said. "We supplied our Crystal glasses for a Canterbury Party last night in exchange for an operation,"

"What operation?" Aden asked.

"The people we gave the supplies to. They have a lot of contacts in Russia and my mother needed an operation on her brain. There is a doctor in Russia that can do the operation. No one else I have access to can,"

Aden nodded. Tyler's mother might have been a psychotic bitch at times but if she needed a medical operation then Aden really hoped she got it.

He pressed down even harder on the pressure points. "Who did you supply the glasses to?"

"If I say then my family will disown me,"

"If you don't tell me you will die," Aden said knowing full well he would never ever kill someone unless he absolutely had to.

He looked at Marcus and he really knew Marcus was judging him but he was beautiful just standing there in that towel. So beautiful.

"Fine," Tyler said. "I only have a name and an address of a company where I personally delivered the glasses to. Olav Redstone of Olav Exports,"

Marcus laughed. "You're kidding, right?"

Aden grabbed some of the scented oils and poured them all over Tyler's back and he moaned in pleasure. Aden was actually surprised the oils were warm for a change. This place really was professional.

Aden made a Lighter sound to scare Tyler, he loved it how Marcus was forcing himself not to laugh.

"Don't," Tyler said like a little girl. "I'm not kidding,"

"What's wrong?" Aden asked.

"Olav Exports is a major international front with billions of pounds of investment in the UK," Marcus said.

"Good so you can siege their accounts," Aden said.

"No. According to the Government the UK relies too much on the investment for us to siege it but at least we have a name," Marcus said.

Tyler kicked Aden.

He fell backwards.

Tyler pushed up.

Whipping out a pistol.

Marcus flew forward.

Punching Tyler in the jaw.

Aden ran forward.

Kicking Tyler in the jaw.

Tyler was out cold but Aden didn't want to leave a criminal leader that tried to kill them both breathing. His father had taught him a lot over the years and one of his biggest lessons was that if an enemy leaves alive then they will come after you again and again until one of you is dead.

Aden looked at the various scented oils and other massage chemicals on the little table and he picked them up. They were all toxic if swallowed so he poured them all into Tyler's mouth and nose and just left him there to die.

As him and Marcus left the room he made sure that Marcus left first in case he had the stupid idea to try and save Tyler without him knowing.

Aden led them down the long corridor back out into the main steam room. "It looks like we're working together now,"

"Really?" Marcus asked laughing. "I'm a government official. You're a criminal. We don't work together,"

"That might be true in normal times but you have government resources and I have my criminal network. And I am sure your government wants Blackout back as much as I do?"

"What's in it for you?"

Aden grinned because he really did hate lying to such a kind, beautiful and cute man but he was going to have to.

"I get to spend a little more time with you,"

"And I know that isn't it but I trust you wouldn't kill me for now,"

"Try ever," Aden said meaning every single word of it.

Aden held the door open for Marcus and now he couldn't believe he was finally working with a beautiful man from MI5 that he would have to deal with at some point. But he meant what he said, *he* would never kill Marcus and he seriously hoped he could keep the rest of his family from doing the same.

An impossible wish if there ever was one.

CHAPTER 9
7th May 2023
London, England

As much as Marcus never ever intended to take sexy Aden back to MI5, he was perfectly okay taking him to the small MI5 safe house that him and Jessica had been using as their unofficial base of operations for a little while and it was the perfect place to hopefully get some prints off Aden.

Not that he believed Aden was stupid enough to fall for any of their tricks for a moment.

Marcus led hot as hell Aden into their little London apartment with great views overlooking all the top London landmarks and the River Thames as it swirled, twirled and churned around itself. Marcus really liked that Jessica had cleaned the apartment a lot so even the dark wooden floors shone a little and the bright white cabinets and walls dazzled in the late morning sun.

There was even three piping hot mugs of coffee

on the round dining table for them to enjoy but Marcus didn't like it how Jessica's computer was running and she wasn't about.

Then the toilet flushed and Jessica came out behind them and went back over to her computer. Marcus had to admit she looked great with her shortish blond hair that was a little messy but done in a really stylish way and her slim-fitting black dress made her look great.

He still couldn't believe she didn't have a boyfriend. A lot of men were seriously missing out.

"Nice you finally joined us," Jessica said as she stood up again and offered Aden a hug.

Aden laughed. "Oh cool you're holding a pin-tracking device on your index finger of your left hand. Is that the old version or the newer version with a 200-metre listening capability?"

Marcus just laughed because he was seriously starting to fall for Aden. He was smart, beautiful and he seemed to know everything.

"Maybe the newer version," Jessica said like a child that had just been told off so she put it down and offered the hug again.

Aden smiled. "If we're going to hug then get rid of the two small listening devices on your left arm that come off the moment they touch my clothes. There is another small red dot on your dress that is something. And I don't doubt there is something else you're hiding,"

"Can we please keep him? He is amazing,"

Jessica asked.

Marcus laughed because he would have been perfectly happy keeping such a sexy man with him at all times. But he was surprised and rather impressed that Aden knew so much about spyware and whatnot. It wasn't normal to know *this* much, so he couldn't workout what exactly Aden's family was in to.

"What have you got on Olav Exports?" Marcus asked.

Jessica sat down at her computer. "Three main offices in Europe, the UK and Asia. Olav himself has been connected to over three hundred deaths and assassination attempts and there is even evidence he's murdered entire villages in Asia so he could expand his poppy farm,"

"He's a drug dealer," Marcus said.

"Exactly," Jessica said, "but he came to the attention of MI5 last year when he killed two of our officers in broad daylight after Border Force captured three million pounds worth of Heroin entering the country. And he funds three main terrorist organisations that focus on the UK,"

Marcus shook his head. They really needed to take Olav out and destroy his entire network all over the world but sadly that wasn't his job as an MI5 officer. His job was just to protect the UK no matter the cost.

"Why does he want Blackout then?" Aden asked.

"I don't know," Marcus said. "It doesn't seem normal for him to want something that… oh,"

Marcus couldn't believe he had been so stupid because he now understood exactly why Olav wanted Blackout. If he was that annoyed at Border Force for stopping his Heroin getting into the country then the easiest way to get revenge would be to knockout the UK's entire power network including their secure systems.

Meaning Olav could literally just fly the Heroin in without it even being registered and Olav definitely had the means to get missiles for the attack on the Hall. A simple flight during a blackout would be easy for the likes of him.

So Marcus told Aden and Jessica all of this.

"Bring up a chair kids," Jessica said smiling and grabbing her cup of coffee. "We have to do some research and we have to find Olav before he strikes,"

Marcus couldn't agree more and he just grinned as Aden picked up the coffee mug. Maybe he would know exactly who the hot sexy man was sooner than he ever thought possible.

Little did Marcus realise he was going to have the shock of his life the moment he found out.

CHAPTER 10
7th May 2023
London, England

Aden was flat out impressed that an organisation as poorly run, smelly and almost pointless as MI5 could actually afford a safehouse or safe-apartment as nice as this one. This was a lot better with its great views, cleanliness and good white cabinets compared to the one him and Isabella had stayed in last night.

It was just impressive.

Aden rather liked sitting at the dining table with Jessica typing around on her computer, each key press making a tapping sound that echoed off the smooth walls of the apartment. And it was really cosy with the warming, bitter hints of coffee filling the air.

Aden could hardly judge Marcus for wanting to use the cup for his fingerprints but MI5 wouldn't find anything or even if they did everything would done be by the time they found out who his father was and what items he might have given to his father in the past.

He was running a search through his various criminal social media groups about if anyone had seen Olav in recent days and if anyone wanted to kill him. It might have been a risky move but he had to prove to Marcus that he was serious about finding Olav and seriously about how cute he was.

Marcus was just sitting at the table too with one leg over the other humming lightly to himself a merry little tune that Aden didn't recognise. It was rather sweet seeing Marcus relaxed for a change as he too ran a search.

"What you know Jess?" Marcus asked.

"Not very well. I've running Olav through every single private and public camera in the entire UK to find him,"

"Is that legal?" Aden asked not knowing why he cared.

"Nope because we technically need a warrant to search through private footage but what the UK public doesn't know won't hurt them,"

Aden smiled because that was such a lie. The UK Public doesn't know that Blackout could be used to knock out every single electronic product in the entire country and that would hurt them a lot.

"I'm out of leads," Marcus said. "Looks like it's all down to you Jess,"

Aden had no idea why Marcus didn't believe in him and his sources but he really wanted to spend a little bit of time just getting to know what Marcus was like, what was his past and why did he do what he did.

And he really just wanted an excuse to talk to him, he was so cute today.

"How did you join the Service?" Aden asked.

Marcus smiled and looked at Jess who nodded, Aden found that a little weird. Maybe Jessica was his boss or more senior than him or maybe it was a sign that Marcus wanted Jessica to be careful in case Aden was searching for information. Whatever it was Aden knew he had to be very, very careful here.

"About five years ago when I was 18 my mother and father died in a car crash. It wasn't anything that normal because the van driver was a terrorist who was escaping from driving into a high street filled with people,"

Aden reached for Marcus's hand out of instinct and he was so glad he let him take it. He really liked how warm, smooth and nice it felt to hold Marcus's hands in his own.

"I'm so sorry," Aden said, "I didn't know but it's a pain losing family. I was abandoned when I was a kid barely ten years old so my now-father found me and loved me,"

"And made you into a criminal," Jessica said.

"I simply get items for him. Whatever he does with the items is his business," Aden said firmly and he really didn't understand why MI5 was so interested in *his* history when they had Olav to deal with.

"Did you never really know your parents?" Marcus asked.

Aden was about to answer when he realised how caringly, lovingly and kindly he had asked. No one had ever said something that nice to him before and no one, besides his father, had cared enough about him to ask.

That only made Aden like Marcus even more. He was so perfect.

"I still have some memories of them and they did love me a lot. I don't really know why they abandoned me and I still look them up online at times. They're successful bankers in London now worth millions of pounds,"

"Oh,"

Aden held Marcus's hands even tighter. "It's okay. I have a comfortable, good life with a family that loves me,"

"If they loved you then why are you alone?" Jessica asked as she typed more on her laptop.

Aden forced himself to relax. He really didn't want her or Marcus suspecting that Isabella wasn't watching his every move, she was actually one of the people he was waiting to reply.

As soon as Isabella or his father contacted him Aden knew that it would be all systems go and then his father and his forces would descend on Olav's location *after* they were there so he could just take Blackout without Aden having to steal it from MI5.

He just wanted Marcus to be kept safe. That was his only concern.

"I am more than capable of looking after

myself," Aden said hoping that be enough for Jessica.

"Fair enough," Marcus said. "Do you have a boyfriend?"

"Enough," Jessica said. And Aden finally realised exactly what that nod had been about earlier, it was good to know Marcus was more than interested in him and he had been concerned he might tell Aden too much.

Hence why Jessica had to make sure he was behaving himself.

Aden kissed Marcus's hands and grinned as Isabella texted him back with a location for Olav. So he wiped his fingerprints off the mug and was looking forward to telling Marcus where they were going.

"He's at a farmhouse in Yorkshire," Aden said. "I'll send you the address now,"

"Wait," Jessica said standing up. "How can we trust you and your source?"

"You don't have an option unless you have better information," Aden said coldly.

Aden loved it as Jessica frowned and nodded and Aden knew that everything was going to plan.

But his stomach tightened into a painful knot as he realised his hope and dream of making sure Marcus didn't get hurt might be a lot harder than he ever thought possible.

Especially with Isabella watching his every move.

CHAPTER 11
7th May 2023
Yorkshire, England

As the fiery sun started to set and set the sky ablaze in a firestorm of red, pink and orange, Marcus leant on the cold flint wall of the property in his full tactical gear.

He was really impressed with the tall green hills all around him that were thankfully clear of enemies and he was pleased that Olav's security seemed to be third-world at best because he couldn't see any guards about.

Out in front of him was a few hundred metres of long thick green grass that probably would have come up to Marcus's knees and led towards a massive brown farmhouse like it had been picked up from the American South and just landed in Yorkshire like it had been transported by aliens. There were no clear signs of security, no cameras and no signs of life except for the lights were on in the house.

None of this made any sense but judging by the road markings and the tyre tracks on the road, Marcus didn't doubt there had been a lot of movement lately. They had either just missed them completely or something else was happening.

Marcus took out his two Glocks and smiled as beautiful, sexy Aden took out his knives. He almost couldn't believe he had almost asked if Aden had a boyfriend or not but he really, really wanted to know.

In this line of work it was just impossible to meet men as beautiful, hot and sexy as Aden and Marcus didn't want to leave him at the end of this mission. He felt a strange connection to Aden that went way beyond attraction, it was nice talking to him and learning about him and his past.

And it only made Marcus fall in love with him even more.

"Come in," Jessica said over his earpiece.

"We're here," Marcus said. "No signs of life. Does the satellite have anything?"

"Sort of. It seems there are life signs in the farmhouse maybe ten guys so be careful. I would recommend waiting until dark,"

Marcus was surprised that Aden looked a little panicked by that realisation but he didn't blame him. There was nowhere near to rest and watch the farmhouse except for this stretch of road. And each moment they were out here the greater chance there was of being discovered.

This wasn't ideal.

"We're going to breach now," Marcus said.

"Confirmed," Jessica said. "And Aria wants me to remind you that Blackout is the prize here. Nothing else matters,"

"Okay," Marcus said looking at the beautiful man standing next to him.

"Let's go," Aden said.

Marcus hopped over the flint wall and couldn't believe that he had jumped straight into a pile of cow shit and seriously didn't smell grand.

Aden laughed and Marcus shook his head as they crouched down low to blend into the grass and they went towards the farmhouse.

The key for these sorts of missions was to always be silent, careful and completely aware of the surroundings. Marcus hated hearing stories about his friends being killed because they didn't see a landmine or a guard opening the door.

Marcus kept going forward.

It was even worse on this mission because all Marcus wanted to do was keep Aden safe. He wanted to date him so he couldn't date a corpse.

Marcus noticed a door was opening up ahead that led out onto a patio area.

Marcus stopped immediately and ducked into the long thick grass. There was a tall woman in a white business blouse, trainers and trousers. She lit up a smoke.

He looked at Aden close behind him and he shook his head Aden was already lining up one of his knives to kill her.

Marcus wasn't completely against it but they did have a mission to do. Each death would only increase the risk of detection.

"Hello?" the woman asked.

Marcus looked at the woman and was so relieved she was on the phone to someone and she was distracted.

He gestured they continue on and make sure that they weren't seen. He was still impressed as hell at how artful, elegant and stunning Aden was as he moved through the entire grass field without making a single sound.

Marcus really couldn't imagine doing the same.

When they were on the very edge of the long thick grass Marcus stopped and the woman was still standing there on her phone just clicking through stuff. She was still distracted but she wasn't talking to anyone.

Marcus hated it as Aden whistled and the woman came over.

Then like an angel of death Aden grabbed the woman and killed her before she could even register what was happening.

Marcus smiled when he noticed the woman was carrying a lot of knives herself. She was a guard and at least they had just given themselves one less enemy to deal with.

They both stood up and went over to the glass door the woman had walked out of and it was open.

Marcus went inside and he really hoped that this mission wasn't going to be something he was going to regret.

Little did Marcus realise his entire world was about to be turned upside down and not for the reasons he ever expected.

LOVE BETRAYS YOU

CHAPTER 12
7th May 2023
Yorkshire, England

Aden really hadn't wanted to kill that female guard but he seriously wanted this entire affair to just hurry up now because sooner or later his father would be here and he needed that damn Blackout to make sure he didn't fail his father.

It was that simple.

As him and Marcus went through the glass door, he made sure his knives were ready to strike and that he was aware of the three opened doors ahead. They slowly went up the long brown wooden corridor that stuck of cat wee but Aden hadn't heard a cat here so that was always a good sign.

Aden looked in the first door and that was just a small kitchen area that was empty. That was good.

Aden watched as Marcus looked through another door and that was empty and then they both heard the sound of a TV turning on coming from the direction of the third door.

Aden nodded to Marcus to tell him they would storm in there together and thankfully Marcus understood the sign.

They stormed in.

The room was completely empty besides from an armchair, a TV and a webcam that was very much focused on them.

Aden threw a knife at the TV to turn it off and then he threw another at the webcam for good measure. He got the knives back with a simple flick of his wrist.

There was no other way in or out of the room so it made no sense that someone had turned on the TV and managed to escape before they had got there.

Aden went over to one of the long rough block walls and noticed there was a bookcase right in front of where the door would logically be located. He checked the floor and noticed there were cuts in the floor so the bookcase should have swung out.

Marcus held his ear and Aden shook his head as he hated that Jessica was talking to him and for some reason he wasn't able to hear it this time. He really hoped that geeky woman hadn't managed to figure out who his father was.

Not that it mattered because soon he would have Blackout, a proud father and a very safe Marcus. That was all he wanted.

Aden gestured Marcus to come and help him move the bookcase.

"What was that about?" Aden asked quietly as Marcus came over to help him.

"Nothing much just that Jessica noticed a heat signature in the surrounding hills. Maybe a guard or something,"

Aden forced himself not to react. That was probably Isabella finally arriving after being delayed by their father for hours. If she was here as the vanguard then his father and his forces would be here soon.

Aden was running out of time.

They pulled the case with a massive pull and the bookcase swung open and a lot of voices started to become a lot louder.

Marcus fired.

Bullets firing into flesh.

Aden flew at them.

Knives slicing through flesh.

Blood sprayed up walls.

Corpses bleed on the ground.

Painting the floors.

Aden smiled as he looked at his handy work. These idiots never saw what was coming. No one moved on the other side. There were no voices, no sounds of movement and not even any sounds of breathing.

Aden went through to the room the bookcase had been blocking and he carefully poked his head round the edge of the bookcase and there were only three tall men in tight sexy black suits pointing their weapons at his head and Olav was sitting on a sofa like he was in total control of the situation.

Then Aden heard ten more men come in behind them and he just couldn't believe they had been completely outflanked and now they were surrounded.

"Come out from your bookcase," a guard said.

Aden looked at the beautiful man he really wanted to protect more than anything and Marcus nodded at him. Aden still made sure his knives could be thrown the moment they needed to be but he lowered them just enough that an untrained person might stupidly believe they were safe.

"Now then," Olav said in a perfect English accent, "we have a lot to discuss including how the hell the son of a criminal mastermind and an MI5 Officer found me,"

As much as Aden wanted Marcus to be spared of this conversation he knew it was flat out impossible and he had no idea if him or Marcus would be walking out of here alive.

No idea at all.

CHAPTER 13
7th May 2023

Yorkshire, England

Marcus wanted nothing more than to simply shoot all these idiots in the head as they dared to threaten the beautiful man he seriously liked. Marcus was forced to throw his gun over to Olav and then he felt the cold metal barrel of a gun against the back of his head.

He watched as the foul monsters placed another gun barrel at the back of Aden's head too.

All Marcus wanted to do was charge at that particular guard and kill him. It was only now that he was realising how much he liked and wanted to protect to Aden. The mission didn't matter only the sweet, kind man that he almost loved mattered.

"How is your father these days?" Olav asked.

Marcus had no idea who Aden's father was or why the hell he was so well-known but he really wanted to find out. He hoped that Jessica had found something back at the safe house but he doubted it. Aden seemed to be way too smart to leave anything behind.

"Very well thank you," Aden said. "However he is greatly hurt that you have such an item that he is after,"

"Then your father should have spoken to me himself instead of teaming up with this goodie scumbag,"

Marcus laughed. He had been called a lot in his time but that certainly had to be a new one. He looked at the three men next to Olav they were starting to relax now and that made him question why didn't they think Aden was going to kill them and their Master.

"Who is your father?" Marcus asked.

He realised he should have asked that a hell of a lot earlier but maybe Jessica was right maybe he had been too focused on Aden's beauty.

Olav started laughing. Marcus noticed the men were looking uneasily at each other and even the guard behind him dug the gun a little more into his skull.

They clearly weren't used to their boss laughing. And Marcus wasn't sure if that was good or bad.

There wasn't a clear way out of the situation just yet so he needed to do two things. Stay alive long enough to find an escape route and try to find out as much information as possible.

"Jessica," Marcus said quietly in case his earpiece

was still working but he hated how quiet Jessica had been for the last few minutes.

"Don't talk. I'm still here. I can see that you have 13 foes and Olav keeping you at gun point and remember there is that woman in the hills too. Maybe she's another foe,"

Marcus rolled his eyes. This seriously wasn't good news.

"I'll try to get you backup but that won't be for another half an hour,"

All Marcus wanted was some good news and it was just typical that Jessica only ever gave him bad news.

"Why do you want Blackout?" Marcus asked gesturing he wanted to come forward and thankfully Olav let him.

It was even better when the man with the gun in the back of his head didn't follow him. Marcus could start thinking up a way to escape hopefully.

"Blackout is the future of mass casualty warfare," Olav said. "Sure bombs, missiles and suicide bombers are highly effective weapons for mass destruction but, I ask you this MI5, why should I use weapons against a society when I can simply cause a society to kill itself?"

Marcus didn't understand exactly what he meant for a few moments. Then he realised just how twisted and stupid Olav really was.

"You mean to tell me that if you knocked out a country's or a good few of them and their electronic systems. Then security, computer and military systems will be down," Marcus said. "That would cause mass destruction, robbery and violence,"

"And better yet," Olav said. "Heads of State like Russia and China and Iran will be paying me handsomely to knock out the systems of their neighbours. The Russian Empire will be reborn and the New Russian Empire will eclipse the old one,"

"You're insane," Aden said.

Marcus couldn't agree more.

"You two are fools as is your father Aden,"

"Incoming," Jessica said through the earpiece.

Marcus looked at Aden. "You might need to duck,"

A missile screamed through the air.

Marcus and Aden leapt to one side.

Marcus tackled a guard to the ground.

A missile struck the farmhouse.

A wall exploded.

Sending deadly shards into the guards.

A helicopter landed outside.

Marcus punched the guard.

Killing him.

Marcus ripped the gun off his corpse and leapt up.

Six guards got up.

Marcus fired.

He charged.

Aden threw his knives.

They smashed into chests.

Blood poured out of them.

Guards screamed.

Marcus looked around for Olav.

He started to run away.

Marcus shot him in the knee.

And when Marcus went over to see him he saw exactly what he wanted, on Olav's bloody right wrist was Blackout or at least the command part of the larger system.

Marcus took it off his wrist and grinned. He was surprised that such a tiny watch-like device could destroy entire countries and bring down governments and usher in a brand-new age of tyranny. He was almost tempted to annihilate it there and then to make sure that no one could ever use it.

But he had his orders and he had to get this back to MI5 before something bad happened.

"Wow," Aden said, "that's Blackout. Can I hold it?"

Marcus just grinned at the beautiful man. Aden was so cute and sweet and clever as he stood there smiling. Marcus really couldn't have done this without him and as Olav started laughing next to him, Marcus nodded and passed him Blackout.

It wasn't like Aden was going to run off with it, use it or actually do anything with it. Marcus trusted Aden and after the chaos of the past two days he didn't doubt that Aden would ever betray him.

"Excellent work little brother," a woman said.

Marcus jumped as the woman from the hall went

over to Aden and hugged him tight.
>What the fuck was happening?
>He had killed her. Surely?

CHAPTER 14
7th May 2023
Yorkshire, England

Aden absolutely hated the entire damn situation as he felt Isabella's wonderfully warm arms around him. There were still little pieces of ash floating down and some of the farmhouse on the other side was on fire and the smell of smoke and charred flesh filled the air.

Aden hated seeing Marcus's look of horror form on his beautiful face as he realised what was happening. Aden had never wanted this to happen or anything else, he had only ever wanted to protect, save and maybe even love Marcus a little bit.

It was clear that was never ever going to happen and it was all his fault. At least this would now be the end and Marcus wouldn't have to see him again.

"What does it feel like?" Isabella asked like a kid in a candy store.

Aden rubbed the perfectly smooth black metal of

the watch in his hands and it felt good and really nice. He felt powerful, rich and like he could do anything. Mostly he was just glad that his father would be proud of him but holding Blackout did make him feel good.

"My turn little brother," Isabella said.

"Was this the plan all along?" Marcus asked.

Aden shook his head. "I did this to protect you actually,"

"My son really did do it all to save you," a man said with a deep, booming voice.

Aden jumped at the sound of his father and his stomach tightened into a painful knot. He really hoped his father was proud of him and that nothing bad was going to happen.

"Count Harrad of the Crimson Gauntlet Crime Family," Marcus said. "Responsible for the murder of fifty people, the sales of tens of millions of pounds' worth of black market weaponry and so many more crimes I don't know where to start,"

Aden shrugged. He wasn't that bothered by what other business arrangements his father got up to because his father loved him more than his real parents ever had. His father was a good man, a questionable man at times but he was a good man at heart.

His father came over and took Blackout from Isabella and he kissed *her* of all people on the head and not him.

"I got Blackout for you father," Aden said like a

child.

"I know," his father said getting out his characteristic golden gun and pointing it at Marcus.

"Wait," Aden said. "Father we cannot kill him. We have to escape now and make sure that MI5 don't track us,"

Aden really had no damn idea why his father wanted to be such an idiot about this. They couldn't kill Marcus, he was such a good person, such a beautiful man and Aden didn't want to live in a world without him even if they weren't dating.

"Can I please kill him dad?" Isabella asked. "I can make it painful, like super painful,"

Aden looked at Marcus and he could see the shock, the betrayal and the sheer look of horror in his eyes. He hated that Marcus had to see this and experience it.

He wasn't sure how to protect the man that he wanted to fuck so badly besides from doing the extreme, but maybe that was the only way to save Marcus. And maybe bring down his father at the same time.

Aden shook the stupid idea away because he just couldn't betray his father. His father was totally a good man at heart, he was loving and Aden forced himself to think of another lie.

He just didn't want his father to kill Marcus.

"Let's take him with us," Aden said. "He's an MI5 Intelligence officer inside his head is a whole bunch of state secrets that we can sell to our friends, his enemies,"

Aden subtly winked at Marcus but he had no idea if Marcus knew he was doing this out of some twisted love. Marcus probably didn't because intelligence officers could be so thick at times.

"Sure," his father said. "I have the Head of the Russian Federal Security Services arriving tomorrow morning anyway. We can hand him over then as well for extra resources,"

Aden didn't know how much better any of this was but it proved that Marcus might live to see another day.

"Come on," his father said. "We're going back to the chopper before MI5 shows up. Make sure our guest is knocked out and alive for now,"

Aden smiled as a guard knocked out Marcus and he was so relieved that Marcus was alive.

Then Isabella came so close to him that Aden could feel her breathe on his ear. "But just remember that I love killing at night and whenever I fancy it. I wonder how long your boyfriend will last before I go cut, slice and bang on him,"

Aden forced out a laugh because that was what she was expecting but now Aden realised he absolutely had to save the man he loved.

And sadly he did actually love Marcus, as annoying as that realisation was.

CHAPTER 15
8th May 2023

Unknown Location, United Kingdom or Rest of World

The thick smells of petrol, burning rubber and charred flesh filled the air as Marcus finally woke up. He had no idea how long he had been out, he didn't know where he was and now all he wanted in the entire world was to know what the hell had just happened.

He flat out couldn't believe that Aden had betrayed him so badly. And he had been stupid enough to let that little traitor into his mind, heart and soul.

Marcus took a long deep breath of the awful air and made himself focus on his surroundings. He could focus on the bloody traitor later but for now he just had to survive. The UK was doomed if he distracted himself for too long.

The pitch darkness of wherever he was might

have limited what he could see but Marcus was more than glad he had been in dark places before. His other senses became heightened and they allowed him to focus more on other features of the environment.

There was a loud deafening hum and bang and pop all around him but it seemed to be focused behind him. Marcus recognised the little sound from his days exploring ferries with his brother when they should have been above deck.

Marcus loved getting into trouble with Ryan.

He wasn't sure why he was on a ship or ferry but that would make sense. It would certainly explain why no one had never managed to find Harrald's base of operations.

It was because it was always moving from one city to another city via the oceans and sea. Damn Harrald and his criminal family.

Marcus tried to move his fingers slightly but he couldn't. They felt tied to something and the rough texture told him that he was *only* bound with thick rough rope that dug into his wrists the more he struggled.

He knew he shouldn't have been surprised at all by the skill of Harald's men and women but he still was. He was more surprised that such a brilliant and sexy man like Aden was working with him but that was just an annoying detail.

Marcus tried to find the knot but he couldn't.

He tried to move his feet but they tied even tighter onto the chair and he wasn't even sure that was correct. He only knew he was tied onto something cold, hard and something that didn't allow him to move.

The lights exploded on.

Marcus closed his eyes for a brief moment as his eyes adjusted to the bright white light all around him. Why couldn't criminals just have nice dim lights for their guests? It was so damn rude of them.

Marcus shook his head as he saw that Isabella woman walk towards him in-between the tall metal crates filled with guns, bombs and other weapons if their labels were to be believed. He doubted it but still.

He supposed Isabella wasn't a bad looking woman in her black military gear but it was her eyes that concerned him. They were hungry, deranged and they were looking at Marcus like how he used to look at twinks when he was a new outed man that wanted to experience all the pleasures of gay society.

He had both loved and hated his whore era in equal measure despite how sensational the sex was.

"My little brother likes you a lot," Isabella said taking out a knife.

"He is hot," Marcus said wanting to buy himself as much time as possible to escape. He didn't know why but he seriously had a sense that Aden was going to save him at some point but until then Marcus had to try to save himself.

"Do you love him?"

"I don't know. I've always found that word a

little hard to say myself. What about you Isabella, have you ever loved someone?"

"Of course," she said scratching the edge of the knife against a metal crate. "I have loved many, many men and then I have killed them all. I am very much a one night stand sort of girl,"

"More like a one-night kill sort of girl," Marcus said grinning.

Isabella clapped. "Oh you are a goodie. I will enjoy killing you. How about we start with a chopped finger or something? Maybe even a little toe,"

"I thought your father said to keep me alive and intact for the FSB coming later on," Marcus said. "Would you really want to disobey your father?"

"My father will be dead soon anyway and once I have killed him then everything will be mine and everything you have come to love will be burnt to the ground," Isabella said smiling.

Marcus gulped because he might have had a way to destroy this organisation from the inside but he needed someone on his side. He doubted that Aden would do anything that might cause a conflict between him and Isabella even if it meant keeping his father alive.

Marcus really needed to escape sooner rather than later and warn Aden. There was about to be a civil war within this organisation and Marcus really didn't want Aden to suffer.

Even though that was basically impossible at this point.

"Isabella return to the bridge," a man said.

Marcus smiled at her. "When you return at least have the decency to fight me in a combat before you start hacking me up,"

Isabella gave him a little bow and then she went away.

Marcus started pulling harder and harder on the ropes because he seriously needed to be free before she got back.

Otherwise the idea of him letting Aden suffer in this civil war scared him a lot more than he ever wanted to admit.

CHAPTER 16
8th May 2023

Twenty Miles Off The English Coast

Aden seriously hated himself as he leant against the icy coldness of the metal walls of the square bridge as he waited for Isabella of all people to join them in the Bridge. The white sterile walls reflected the bright white lights of the bridge perfectly and only made it seem brighter compared to the sheer darkness of the world outside.

Aden could barely see where the black water started and the pitch darkness of the sky stopped. It was that dark outside and with the five women in their blue uniforms wiping the sleep from their eyes, Aden couldn't blame them for feeling so tired.

He had managed to grab some sleep earlier in the evening but he hadn't really slept too much. He felt so guilty about Marcus and everything that was happening and he was seriously starting to doubt the sheer wisdom of his father.

Aden had always known his father was a sort of bad man but he could see and hear the sheer anger and rage in Marcus' voice about the crimes his father had facilitated. All those innocent lives lost, but still his father couldn't be that bad considering he had raised him when no one else wanted him?

He shook the silly thought away and looked at his father in his full-captain uniform that made him look like a military officer for a moment. His father was leaning against a wooden table filled with maps and whatnot about their current destination.

Then Blackout was on his wrist.

"How does it work Dad?" Aden asked.

Aden loved it as his father smiled how Aden liked to imagine a loving father would grin at his son when he made them extra proud.

"Simple son," his Father said as he gestured him over to his side and pointed to all the dials and buttons on the watch-like device. "You simply click this button to activate it and then you keep moving the dials until they lock onto the Satellite network that Blackout runs on,"

"Then you simply programme Blackout to hit an area and then the world burns," Isabella said as she came in.

Aden hated how his Father immediately started hugging Isabella instead of him. All Aden wanted was a nice friendly hug from his father but clearly that was never going to happen.

"Here's the woman of the hour," his father said.

"This is the woman that made all of this possible,"

Isabella grinned. "Thank you. It wasn't easy having to suggest and escort Aden round like a little dog but I managed to train him,"

"You see son if you keep learning from your sister you will rule this organisation one day instead of her,"

Aden took a few steps back when he saw the sheer rage and anger in her eyes. And Aden realised that Isabella wanted him dead. She didn't love him, she didn't like him, she didn't even value him.

His corpse was all she had ever wanted.

"Father get away from her," Aden said getting out one of his knives.

The female crew in the bridge stood up and aimed his pistols at him.

"What's going on?" his Father said.

But it was too late.

A shot went off and the bullet screamed through his Father's chest and his Father's corpse slumped to the ground.

Then all the women focused their weapons on Aden and Isabella started laughing.

"I actually didn't intend to do all this for another year but Blackout gives me such an opportunity. I could have the likes of the West, China and Russia all bow down to me like a Goddess,"

"You're crazy," Aden said.

"Of course I am but I am a crazy woman with a weapon capable of rebuilding the world in my image.

Once I knock out the West's electronic systems then China will march. And then I will be the Ruler or a Governor in the New Chinese Empire,"

Aden shook his head. Not only because of the sheer craziness of his sister's words but because he actually believed them. He knew that Isabella was a soft mark for anyone clever enough to find the right lie and then Aden realised that his entire life had been a lie too.

His father had never loved him. He had been homeless, desperate and lonely on the streets so whenever anyone would come and show him the smallest amount of kindness he would be all over them.

Aden supposed it had never been hard for Harald to groom him and make him one of his sons just like all the other vulnerable people in the organisation.

"What now?" Aden asked.

Isabella grinned. "Crew turn this ship around and when the FSB chopper gets within range shoot it down and make sure it looks like the West did it,"

"No," Aden said. "That's insane. If Russia and China believe the West assassinated the head of their intelligence service then it could easily start World War Three,"

"Exactly. Then coupled with the Blackout on the West that will happen a few hours later it will simply look like the East is taking revenge. And then World War Three will start and the West will lose,"

"Bastard," Aden said.

"Because we have had some good times together little brother I will give you ten minutes and hide and then I will hunt you down. And kill you,"

"You know exactly where I'm going,"

Isabella just grinned. "Tick tock little mouse,"

Aden ran out the Bridge and seriously hoped he could get Marcus to help save him before they were killed.

And the fate of the world was doomed.

CHAPTER 17
8th May 2023
Twenty-Two Miles Off The English Coast

Marcus had to admit whoever tied these knots were flat out amazing because he could not get out of these knots at all. He had already felt the ship move so something was clearly happening and that only made him want to escape even more.

The heavy metal door to the room opened and Marcus's eyes widened when he saw beautiful sexy Aden run towards him with his knives out.

"Hello traitor," Marcus said without meaning to.

Aden didn't talk as he cut Marcus free and normally if it was anyone else he would have punched, kicked and got the man in a headlock. But he forced himself not to.

Aden might have been a traitor but Marcus didn't doubt there was a good reason for all of it.

"I know I have no right to ask this but I need your help,"

"Three words," Marcus said.

"Isabella in charge. World War Three. Blackout being used,"

Marcus rolled his eyes. It wasn't exactly three words but he would take it because if that psychotic bitch was in charge then something had gone seriously wrong.

And they had to stop it.

Marcus went over to the metal crates all around him and opened them. They were all empty and Marcus supposed that was fair. It would have been a little stupid leaving him with crates full of weapons.

A man exploded through the door.

He fired his gun.

Marcus jumped behind some crates.

Aden threw a knife.

And as the man went down Marcus went straight over to him and picked up the idiot's weapon. He didn't have a lot of shots left but Marcus just wanted to survive.

All whilst keeping Aden safe at the same time.

"We have to kill Isabella," Marcus said, "and get Blackout back,"

"No," Aden said. "Blackout is too powerful for any country or power to have. We have to make sure Blackout is destroyed forever,"

Marcus hated the idea of that. His bosses were going to be so annoyed but he just focused on Aden's soft beautiful lips and realised he might be right.

He touched his earpiece and hoped beyond hope

that Jessica was still there.

"Come in Jessica," Marcus said.

A small amount of static filled his ear so there was still a signal but it was too weak to broadcast.

"We have to get to higher ground then we can call in a naval strike," Marcus said, "and get rid of this ship forever,"

Aden nodded.

A woman stormed in.

Marcus shot the woman in the head.

He gestured they needed to go now because they were sitting ducks in this room.

Marcus opened the heavy metal door and made sure the little metal ship corridor was clean. For a change it was.

He led him and Aden out of the room and from what he knew about ships they needed to turn left and keep going forward.

Marcus kept his gun level in front of him and his wrist relaxed as they went forward. He checked each door and made sure that no one was following them.

No one was.

There was a metal staircase up ahead. A perfect ambush site then Marcus realised the ceiling had turned into a metal grate that allowed him to see who was above them and it made them easier to see.

Bullets screamed down from above.

Marcus jumped forward.

He spun around.

Shooting straight up.

Two corpses fell to the ground.

Marcus hurried up and led Aden up a staircase and onto another deck. The static in his ear was getting a little louder but it still wasn't good enough to broadcast.

"Stop!" a woman shouted.

Aden threw a knife into her neck and retrieved it as they moved past the corpse.

Marcus was really pleased he was with him. They turned around two corners and went into a massive dining hall and then the entire crew stood up, aimed their guns at them and Marcus just laughed.

"You could have warned me," he said to Aden.

"I haven't been on his ship in months. I forget,"

And as much as Marcus wanted to believe that this was just yet another case of Aden betraying him he really knew that this wasn't.

All the crew came over to them and took their guns and knives and escorted them to the bridge.

And Marcus just grinned because that would mean there would be less interference with the earpiece and now Marcus was hoping beyond hope he could contact Jessica.

At least in time to save the world.

CHAPTER 18
8th May 2023

Ten Miles off The Coast Of France

Aden seriously hated how the icy coldness of the gun barrel was being rammed into his back as the dumb crew escorted him and beautiful Marcus into the Bridge. He wasn't even sure why Isabella of all people wanted them alive but at least it gave them another shot to escape.

"I didn't want them here," Isabella said as she hunched herself over the wooden table filled with charts and maps and all sorts of other wonders that Aden would have been more happy burning.

Anything if it meant Isabella would suffer.

Aden looked at Marcus and noticed he was focusing on something. He knew he still had his earpiece but Aden wasn't sure how it worked and would the sign even be picked up this far off the English coast.

He really hoped it was.

Aden looked at the three female crew members that were controlling the ship and doing all sorts of things Aden didn't understand. But he knew they were the key, if he could only damage the controls then maybe that would stop Isabella from doing something.

Or maybe that would destroy the ship and Blackout with it.

"But we did want them here," the crew said.

Aden was surprised when the crew member took the gun out of his back and pointed it at Isabella. A few other people gasped.

Aden had no idea how far the corruption and turncoats spread but it was clear a real civil war was about to happen. He didn't need to know the winner because whoever took over his father's operation would be just as monstrous as he was.

Everyone had to die here.

Aden didn't care anymore about his brother and sisters that were just as bad and vulnerable and groomed as he was. They were all bad people and they all had to die so they couldn't hurt another soul.

"See Isabella," Aden said, "this is what you've caused. You killed the only man that could ever unite everyone under his banner. The Crimson Gauntlet was a Crime Family of power, riches and influence and you have just killed that,"

"Of course," Isabella said. "That's the point because I have always lied about my plan,"

Aden laughed. Isabella was always full of

surprises as she revealed Blackout was on her wrist and the watch-like device was humming, vibrating and fizzing a little.

"You've connected to the main systems," Marcus said. "That's impossible,"

"Nothing is impossible dear boy if you simply forget about the rules of man,"

Aden noticed there was something in the distance. It looked like naval ships or something and that meant they were running out of time to escape.

"Ah yes," Isabella said. "Some stupid Naval ships are coming. Let me give you a small demonstration of my power,"

Isabella clicked Blackout and Aden didn't feel anything but he simply focused on the five Royal Navy ships coming towards them.

He noticed the ships start to slow before it looked like one was trying to turn but the water caught it at the wrong angle and it hit another ship then another then another.

Two ships flipped over and the other three sunk as they smashed into each other.

"All those lives now dead," Aden said. "You are exactly our Father's daughter,"

Bullets screamed through the air.

All the crew that were pointing their weapons at Isabella were dead. Their corpses landed with a thud.

"There is no support for the likes of you anymore," Isabella said as she clicked Blackout a final time. "That's it,"

Aden went forward but a man gripped his arm. "What's it?"

"The Final Command has been issued. Unless you can deactivate it or your MI5 friends can stop Blackout. The full power of Blackout will be unleashed in ten minutes. It will knock out all power in Europe and the UK,"

"Allowing Russia and China to storm through the continent within days," Marcus said.

"Exactly," Isabella said.

Aden shook the man's grip free as he watched Isabella go over to the massive windows as she smiled at the sea around her.

"There is no chance of you saving the day. Not this time," Isabella.

"Let's see about that," Aden said stomping on a guard's foot.

He screamed.

Aden grabbed his gun. Shooting him in the head.

Marcus charged forward.

Aden fired at the windows.

The windows shattered.

Marcus tackled Isabella.

They both fell out the window together.

CHAPTER 19
8th May 2023
Somewhere Off The Coast of France

Marcus hissed as he leapt with Isabella out the window of the bridge and they zoomed towards the immense ground below them.

The grey metal floor zoomed into view and Marcus just focused on making sure Isabella landed first.

She kicked him midair.

Marcus fell away from her.

He saw the ground getting close with shipping containers coming up.

Marcus shot out his hands.

He gripped the edge of one. The sheer force jerked him making him let go.

He fell to the ground.

When he landed with a thud Marcus hissed in pain as it pulsed up his legs and the rest of his entire body. He was surprised he was actually alive but that meant Isabella was alive too.

Static filled his ears and Marcus just knew his damn earpiece was broken now and he was completely alone with Isabella stalking the shipping containers.

Marcus went to take out his gun but realised he didn't have one. Those dumb crew members had taken his one earlier.

Isabella's laughter echoed all around him. It got louder and louder.

Marcus ducked.

A fist shot past him.

Marcus spun around.

Isabella punched him in the jaw.

He slammed into a shipping container.

She kicked him.

Again. Again.

Ramming his head into the shipping container.

Marcus collapsed to the ground.

Marcus grabbed her foot.

Pulling it to one side.

She fell.

Marcus jumped on top of her.

She slashed him with his nails.

Cutting into his skin.

Marcus screamed in pain.

She headbutted him.

Punched him.

Kicked him.

Marcus fell to one side.

Isabella got up and pressed one of her boots into his throat making Marcus gag a little.

"I had so much hope for you. I thought you were going to be a good fighter and a worthy kill," Isabella said.

Marcus grabbed her boot and she was surprised by the sheer strength. He lifted the boot off her throat.

She tried to put all her weight on it. Marcus didn't care. He lifted it off his throat.

Marcus threw her to one side.

Marcus leapt up. He flew at her.

Marcus kicked her.

Gripped the back of her head.

He ripped out her hair.

He spun her around.

Aiming her at the shipping container.

She jumped up.

Kicking herself off the shipping container.

Marcus fell backwards.

He hit something.

His vision blurred.

He saw a gun.

He leapt forward.

He smashed into Isabella.

He felt the gun.

Marcus pushed it away from him.

She fired it.

Shots screamed off into the air.

Marcus elbowed her in the ribs.

Isabella kicked him in-between the legs.

Marcus dropped like a stone and as his vision cleared all he could see was Isabella's smiling face that was laughing at him.

Marcus hated the woman. He had no idea how such a stupid woman could be so cold, awful and foul towards other people. He almost pitied her but he had seen what she did to people she didn't like.

She deserved everything she ever got in life.

Isabella pointed her gun at his head. "I'll give you a quick death but I will so enjoy killing my little brother. I will make his death slow and painful so that by the end he is begging for death,"

Marcus just frowned at her. How dare the bitch want to kill that hot sexy man that had given up everything to save him. Sure Aden might have betrayed him. But Aden also freed him, tried to save the world and he had even shot out the window to help him.

That meant something to Marcus and it didn't matter if Aden wasn't typical boyfriend material. In this line of work it didn't matter because Marcus did love Aden.

So he would protect him to the end and that all started with killing this bitch.

Marcus leapt up so quickly the world blurred.

He charged at Isabella.

He gripped her wrists.

His fingernails digging into her flesh.

She screamed in pain.

Marcus whacked the gun from her grip.

He grabbed her head.

Ramming it into the shipping container.

Her head landed with a thud.

She screamed out in pain.

Marcus didn't stop.

He kept whacking her head again and again.

Something cracked. Isabella screamed in agony.

He kept going.

Marcus kept smashing until there was nothing left to smash into the shipping container and his hands were covered in blood and Isabella's corpse landed with a thud.

He knelt down next to the body and carefully took Blackout off her wrist and he felt his stomach twist into a painful knot.

He wasn't a computer expert. He didn't know how to save the world, he didn't know how to deactivate Blackout.

Marcus did the only logical thing he could do in the situation. He placed the watch-like device on the ground and he stomped on it.

Again and again until Blackout was all gone and there was nothing left for anything to use or rebuild.

Marcus couldn't deny he felt a little dead inside considering that he had failed in his mission in more ways than he cared to remember. He hadn't retrieved Blackout and maybe he was a failure in the eyes of MI5 but he just sort of knew he had helped to make the world and the UK a safer place today.

All because no one could ever use Blackout again and at least the world wasn't in danger from a stupid UK defence programme that Marcus seriously didn't believe should have happened in the first place.

Now Marcus just had one more thing to do. He had to talk with the beautiful man he loved and just see if there was a future for them together and he really wanted to prove to himself that love doesn't betray everyone in the end.

CHAPTER 20
8th May 2023
Somewhere off The Coast Of France

As Aden got the last of his knives out of the corpses scattered around the bridge he couldn't believe how his life had changed now and he really didn't know what was going to happen in the future for him. The future was a complete mystery but he supposed it could have been as light or dark as he liked depending on what he wanted for it.

Aden laughed to himself as he leant against the icy coldness of the wall of the bridge. He had never had the chance to think about what he wanted for his future before, he had never wanted to be homeless or abandoned and once his father had found him he had never been given a choice. He had always just done what he was told so he could be "loved", survive and not end up on the streets again.

It really was that simple.

Aden wasn't a massive fan of the strange taste

that formed on his tongue from the salty sea air as it mixed with the iron tang of the vapourised blood in the air. He didn't doubt there would be attacks against them all day because of the odd crew members that had survived but Aden didn't mind.

He didn't want to kill them and he would always give them a choice of getting arrested or dying in a pointless fight. He knew most of them would choose the latter but he still liked himself for wanting to give them a choice.

It was even something his father would have been proud of.

"Hello beautiful," Marcus said as he came in and he placed his gun on the wooden table that was a lot more bloody and covered in corpses than when he had left.

Aden put his knives away and he supposed this was the best time they were going to talk about their future. A future he wanted a lot more than he wanted to admit.

"You look good even without your suit on," Marcus said.

Aden laughed. He couldn't believe how calm, wonderful and breathtaking Marcus was even though they had been through betrayal, attempted murders and international crimes together. Marcus was still the hot, sexy and stunning man that Aden had met two days ago.

"Do you really want to do this? We only met two days ago?" Aden asked.

"I do," Marcus said slowly coming over to him. "Because I've been an intelligence officer for five years now and I know meeting hot, incredible men is seriously hard and I don't want to spend another day alone,"

Aden wasn't sure that was the most romantic thing he had ever heard but he was interested in hearing more.

"Aden, you're a beautiful man and I love you more than anything," Marcus said knowing he wanted to hear more. "I know we have both had our struggles but I believe in you more than you will ever know,"

Aden took a few steps closer to him and placed a loving hand on his arm. He really liked how smooth and warm his arms were against his fingers.

"What's going to happen to me?"

Marcus hugged him gently at first but as Aden wrapped his arms around Marcus's fit body he tightened his arms. So much so that Aden enjoyed the warm feeling of Marcus's breath on his neck.

"I honestly don't know but nothing bad will happen because you helped me. You fixed this and you helped to save everyone. If you tell us everything about your father then I'm sure you won't serve any prison time,"

Aden smiled at that. Marcus, always the hot stunning man that focused on law and order and everything that good citizens did. Aden really did love that about him.

Aden kissed him softly. They might have only met two days ago but Aden really loved the soft, warmth of his lips against his. Marcus was definitely the best kisser he had ever had the pleasure of meeting and he really liked having him in his life.

And he just sort of knew without a shadow of a doubt that whatever happened now until and beyond the time that they were rescued by the French Coastguard that everything would be okay. Aden had Marcus by his side, he had a man who loved him and Aden really, really couldn't believe how lucky he was to have found them.

Life was great and Aden was so looking forward to spending the rest of his life with such a stunning man. And maybe they would even get to travel the UK together protecting the country and fighting side by side.

Now that would be a hell of a lot of fun.

CHAPTER 21
3rd June 2023
London, England

If anyone had asked Marcus if the next month would have been so fun, enjoyable and simply the best month of his life then he would have called them a liar but they would have turned out to be completely correct.

Marcus still couldn't believe how much fun he had had travelling round the UK with beautiful, sexy Aden by his side as they fought to destroy and clean up the rest of Harald's organisation now that it was in complete chaos. They had travelled together killing, loving and laughing along the way from the top of Scotland all the way down to the very southern tip of England.

Marcus hugged the wonderful man he was loving more and more with each passing day as they both sat on a double-seated camping chair as they watched Ryan coach his little football team. There was a big match tomorrow and Marcus knew they were going to absolutely smash it all because Ryan was an amazing coach, brother and person.

Marcus was really impressed with the great weather for a change as the bright intense sun shone down bathing everything in a rich golden light. He was glad the white lines of the huge football pitch had faded just a little otherwise he might have been blinded.

The car park behind him was full of young happy families out with their children and Marcus enjoyed hearing them laughing, screaming with happiness and playing in the distance in the nearby playground.

They were all safe, happy and Marcus loved his job because of it. It was even better they would never ever know what almost happened to them because of Blackout.

Something MI5 might admitted never happened in the first place so Marcus could never be rewarded or punished for destroying the multi-billion-pound project.

Marcus wrapped his arms around wonderful Aden as he whistled and cheered as one of the kids scored his first-ever goal and that was great fun. Marcus hadn't realised that Aden had such a knack for helping children but Marcus supposed he really shouldn't have been surprised.

As the past month had told him over and over, Aden was a very special, resourceful and loving man that really did just want to help everyone who needed it. He had helped a lot of homeless children up in Manchester, he had helped elderly ladies in London and he had helped food banks in Cornwall.

Marcus still understood it himself but maybe that was because he had always had people that loved him surrounding him. Ryan and his sister were great, Aria and Jessica were his work family and now Aden was his boyfriend.

Something that Ryan was extremely pleased about and Marcus was looking forward to actually spending time with his brother more and his own family. Ryan and his family had taken to Aden instantly and Marcus was now almost worried that he wasn't the family favourite anymore.

Not that it mattered much.

Because him and Aden were a couple that loved each other so much that they could handle anything the world could throw at them. It didn't matter if a terrorist attacked, a bomb went off, even missiles couldn't stop them because they had each other. And that seriously did mean something to Marcus.

And he loved Aden for it.

A delightfully warm breeze blew across the football pitch and Marcus grinned as more and more kids kicked the ball into the goal so artfully that he suspected Aden had been secretly teaching them something without him knowing. The kids seemed so happy, Marcus was more than happy with his life and he was so glad that he was sitting next to the man he loved.

Marcus looked behind him as Aria and Jessica got out of the car and they both smiled at him and Marcus just laughed. One day he was finally going to be able to simply enjoy his Saturdays with his brother, the team and Aden but that wasn't today.

And as Marcus said goodbye to the kids and his brother and simply took Aden by the hand off towards their next mission, Marcus couldn't deny his life was amazing and he wouldn't change anything for the entire world. Because Marcus definitely couldn't get better than this.

GET YOUR FREE SHORT STORY NOW!
And get signed up to Connor Whiteley's newsletter to hear about new gripping books, offers and exciting projects. (You'll never be sent spam)

https://www.subscribepage.io/gayromancesignup

About the author:

Connor Whiteley is the author of over 60 books in the sci-fi fantasy, nonfiction psychology and books for writer's genre and he is a Human Branding Speaker and Consultant.

He is a passionate warhammer 40,000 reader, psychology student and author.

Who narrates his own audiobooks and he hosts The Psychology World Podcast.

All whilst studying Psychology at the University of Kent, England.

Also, he was a former Explorer Scout where he gave a speech to the Maltese President in August 2018 and he attended Prince Charles' 70th Birthday Party at Buckingham Palace in May 2018.

Plus, he is a self-confessed coffee lover!

Other books by Connor Whiteley:

Bettie English Private Eye Series
A Very Private Woman
The Russian Case
A Very Urgent Matter
A Case Most Personal
Trains, Scots and Private Eyes
The Federation Protects
Cops, Robbers and Private Eyes
Just Ask Bettie English
An Inheritance To Die For
The Death of Graham Adams
Bearing Witness
The Twelve
The Wrong Body
The Assassination Of Bettie English
Wining And Dying
Eight Hours
Uniformed Cabal
A Case Most Christmas

Gay Romance Novellas
Breaking, Nursing, Repairing A Broken Heart
Jacob And Daniel
Fallen For A Lie
Spying And Weddings
Clean Break

Awakening Love
Meeting A Country Man
Loving Prime Minister
Snowed In Love
Never Been Kissed
Love Betrays You

<u>Lord of War Origin Trilogy:</u>
Not Scared Of The Dark
Madness
Burn Them All

<u>The Fireheart Fantasy Series</u>
Heart of Fire
Heart of Lies
Heart of Prophecy
Heart of Bones
Heart of Fate

<u>City of Assassins (Urban Fantasy)</u>
City of Death
City of Marytrs
City of Pleasure
City of Power

Agents of The Emperor
Return of The Ancient Ones
Vigilance
Angels of Fire
Kingmaker
The Eight
The Lost Generation
Hunt
Emperor's Council
Speaker of Treachery
Birth Of The Empire
Terraforma
Spaceguard

The Rising Augusta Fantasy Adventure Series
Rise To Power
Rising Walls
Rising Force
Rising Realm

Lord Of War Trilogy (Agents of The Emperor)
Not Scared Of The Dark
Madness
Burn It All Down

Miscellaneous:
RETURN
FREEDOM
SALVATION
Reflection of Mount Flame
The Masked One
The Great Deer
English Independence

OTHER SHORT STORIES BY CONNOR WHITELEY

<u>Mystery Short Story Collections</u>
Criminally Good Stories Volume 1: 20 Detective Mystery Short Stories
Criminally Good Stories Volume 2: 20 Private Investigator Short Stories
Criminally Good Stories Volume 3: 20 Crime Fiction Short Stories
Criminally Good Stories Volume 4: 20 Science Fiction and Fantasy Mystery Short Stories
Criminally Good Stories Volume 5: 20 Romantic Suspense Short Stories

Mystery Short Stories:
Protecting The Woman She Hated
Finding A Royal Friend
Our Woman In Paris
Corrupt Driving
A Prime Assassination
Jubilee Thief
Jubilee, Terror, Celebrations
Negative Jubilation
Ghostly Jubilation
Killing For Womenkind
A Snowy Death
Miracle Of Death
A Spy In Rome
The 12:30 To St Pancreas
A Country In Trouble
A Smokey Way To Go
A Spicy Way To GO
A Marketing Way To Go
A Missing Way To Go
A Showering Way To Go
Poison In The Candy Cane
Kendra Detective Mystery Collection Volume 1
Kendra Detective Mystery Collection Volume 2
Mystery Short Story Collection Volume 1

LOVE BETRAYS YOU

Mystery Short Story Collection Volume 2
Criminal Performance
Candy Detectives
Key To Birth In The Past

<u>Science Fiction Short Stories:</u>
Their Brave New World
Gummy Bear Detective
The Candy Detective
What Candies Fear
The Blurred Image
Shattered Legions
The First Rememberer
Life of A Rememberer
System of Wonder
Lifesaver
Remarkable Way She Died
The Interrogation of Annabella Stormic
Blade of The Emperor
Arbiter's Truth
Computation of Battle
Old One's Wrath
Puppets and Masters
Ship of Plague
Interrogation
Edge of Failure

All books in 'An Introductory Series':
Clinical Psychology and Transgender Clients
Clinical Psychology
Careers In Psychology
Psychology of Suicide
Dementia Psychology
Clinical Psychology Reflections Volume 4
Forensic Psychology of Terrorism And Hostage-Taking
Forensic Psychology of False Allegations
Year In Psychology
CBT For Anxiety
CBT For Depression
Applied Psychology
BIOLOGICAL PSYCHOLOGY 3RD EDITION
COGNITIVE PSYCHOLOGY THIRD EDITION
SOCIAL PSYCHOLOGY- 3RD EDITION
ABNORMAL PSYCHOLOGY 3RD EDITION
PSYCHOLOGY OF RELATIONSHIPS- 3RD EDITION
DEVELOPMENTAL PSYCHOLOGY 3RD EDITION
HEALTH PSYCHOLOGY
RESEARCH IN PSYCHOLOGY

LOVE BETRAYS YOU

FORENSIC PSYCHOLOGY
THE FORENSIC PSYCHOLOGY OF THEFT, BURGLARY AND OTHER CRIMES AGAINST PROPERTY
CRIMINAL PROFILING: A FORENSIC PSYCHOLOGY GUIDE TO FBI PROFILING AND GEOGRAPHICAL AND STATISTICAL PROFILING.
CLINICAL PSYCHOLOGY
FORMULATION IN PSYCHOTHERAPY
PERSONALITY PSYCHOLOGY AND INDIVIDUAL DIFFERENCES
CLINICAL PSYCHOLOGY REFLECTIONS VOLUME 1
CLINICAL PSYCHOLOGY REFLECTIONS VOLUME 2
Clinical Psychology Reflections Volume 3
CULT PSYCHOLOGY
Police Psychology

A Psychology Student's Guide To University
How Does University Work?
A Student's Guide To University And Learning
University Mental Health and Mindset

www.ingramcontent.com/pod-product-compliance
Lightning Source LLC
LaVergne TN
LVHW012114070526
838202LV00056B/5726